Time Pirates
Adventure in the Pacific

By John Alexander Lott

Illustrated by Brandon Russon

ISBN: **1542569591**
ISBN-13: **978-1542569590**

DEDICATION

To my three little daydreamers; my favorite adventurers. Make your dreams come true.

CONTENTS

ACKNOWLEDGMENTS

Thank you to Cameron, who came up with the title even before I began to write, and to the talented Brandon Russon. Your gift helped me make the best decision I've made since I dreamed up this series—inviting you to illustrate the adventure!

CHAPTER 1
WELCOME TO THE JUNGLE

Three children were sliding through time, hoping to stop thieves from stealing the world's largest missing treasures. Cameron, Carsen, and Brynlee Biggs were falling through the time tunnel leading them toward a new destination.

Their last adventure was one with very little danger. The sweltering sun in early Phoenix, Arizona proved to be far more deadly than the "Time Pirate" they were following. Tiny, as the kids had called him due to his comically huge hat sitting on top of his laughably small head, turned out to be proof that the larger the animal's head, the smarter they were, and the smaller it was . . . well, Cameron, the oldest, hoped that their luck would continue and that all of the pirates were as dim-witted as Tiny had been. He had an uncomfortable feeling in his stomach that such luck wasn't likely to continue.

The trio of travelers landed with a chorus of mild grunts in a patch of thick ferns and palm leaves. They were quiet, however, because the last time they landed, Tiny overheard their yelps and almost caught them. None of them wanted to let the new pirate know they were there to stop him just yet.

"I think we should look around a little," Cameron suggested. "But stay quiet!"

The others nodded and then followed their big brother as he crept around a big fern in the direction of sunlight they could see up ahead through the trees. Cameron was the first to reach the edge of the forest. When

Carsen and Brynlee joined him, they gasped at what they saw. They were standing on a mountain overlooking the ocean. It was a steep drop-off from where they stood to the blanketed mountainside below.

Everything around them was bright and colorful. The air was thick and humid like it usually was back at home in Nevada City during August. It smelled of flowers and plants, like a greenhouse they went to with their parents every spring when they bought plants for their garden.

"It's beautiful!" Brynlee whispered. "I want to go lay on that beach."

Cameron noticed the beach for the first time. It was a small stretch of sand between the thick vegetation covering most of the island, and the crystal blue ocean. The sand was dark in color, not like California sand.

"I don't think we're in Kansas anymore," Carsen joked.

"Or Phoenix," added Cameron.

The Biggs bunch stood there taking in their surroundings for a moment longer before they turned back to return to their landing spot. Cameron was about to begin talking to his brother and sister about their plan of action, but he thought he heard something or someone coming through the jungle in their direction. He shoved the two younger Biggs' into the middle of a huge fern and followed quickly.

Cameron poked his head up out of the feathery ferns and looked in every direction. The coast was clear but noises were coming from the direction of a pathway leading away from what looked to be a campsite to the side of where they had landed. The boy led his siblings behind the nearest tree just before a thick necked man came into view.

"Thirty days!" the man growled.

Cameron and Carsen wound up their inner springs getting ready to rocket down the pathway as fast as their legs could carry them. The pirate was talking to them! Cameron reached out to grab his little sister to bring her along for the ride. Brynlee, however was less nervous because she could see the man around the trunk of the tree. He wasn't even looking in their direction, and just seemed to be grumbling to himself.

The children listened as the man complained about how long he had been on the island, and how he was afraid he would go crazy before the boat arrived.

Cameron, Carsen, and Brynlee crinkled up their noses as they looked at each other. Each seemed to be thinking the same thing. They thought they were only going to be a few minutes behind the pirate as they had been in Phoenix.

There they had landed so soon after the pirate that he had barely left the little back room of the store when they arrived through the portal. Each one recalled the fear they had when Tiny came back through the door to see what was making the noises he'd heard.

"Here I am talking to myself. Why, you might ask, am I talking to myself? Well, I'll tell you. I am attempting to stave off lunacy!"

"What's 'stave off' mean?" Brynlee whispered to her brothers.

Carsen shrugged

"Delay, slow down, stop from happening," Cameron whispered back. "Now be quiet."

The pirate continued his reasoning, "Sergeant Beam told me that as long as a man can still make sense as he talks to himself, he stands a good chance of not going crazy--even if he has to spend a long time alone and nearly starving!"

Brynlee had a good look at the man from her spot behind some ferns next to the tree where the Biggs' were hiding.

"He doesn't *look* like he's starving," she whispered, watching the somewhat large rear-end of the pirate as he stacked a few pieces of wood he had been carrying.

"BJ!" Cameron whispered harshly. "I love you, Sis, but will you please shush?"

Carsen nodded his agreement.

"It wasn't long ago that I was . . ." the pirate rambled on and on boasting to himself about his service in the military, his training and his 'cat-like' reflexes.

Cameron noticed that he kept rolling his eyes at how cocky the man was. It was starting to hurt. If the man didn't stop talking to himself out loud soon, there would be permanent damage.

Their new target seemed to be packing himself a lunch in a brown and green backpack. Brynlee saw him take a leather pouch off of a low hanging branch and pull several pieces of what looked like jerky out of it.

Carsen noticed a couple of canteens. He remembered the scorching sun in Phoenix and realized he hadn't had a thing to drink in several hours. He licked his dry lips and stared longingly at the water only a few yards away.

The pirate finished loading up his supplies and started off down the trail through the jungle again. Then the Biggs children came out of hiding.

"How can he have been here for a month?" Carsen wondered.

"I don't know, but I'm pretty sure that he will still be going back to the same night we all left from," Cameron replied. "Vanessa doesn't seem like she would like the idea of the other pirates being able to choose their own return dates. She would want control over something like that."

"Of course," Brynlee chimed in. "She's a control freak. And don't forget, she also said something about everything needing to be done in one night. I don't think it matters how long we stay in any time."

Carsen agreed, "As long as we use the locket and wand to return, it should take us back to the next programmed time slot. At least, that's what it sounded like from her description in the mine."

Cameron was thinking. His hand was rubbing his chin the same way he had seen his dad do so many times when he was writing or working on something that required a lot of thought. He smiled at that as he considered the possibility that they could be stranded in the jungle for a long time, if this pirate's ramblings were accurate. They would need to survive somehow.

"I'm kind of hungry," Carsen said.

"Me too," Brynlee admitted. "Do you think he would miss any of that jerky if we took some?

"I'm betting he would unless we took so little that he might consider it just a mistake in counting," Cameron warned.

The trio of time travelers again committed the only actual crime by loading up on bits and pieces of whatever was lying around. Cam just shook his head at the irony. They had to "borrow" the clothes they were wearing and had to leave Phoenix so fast that they couldn't return them to the store. Now they were taking food from someone who was supposed to be the real bad guy.

They found a metal water bottle full to the brim. They each slipped one piece of dried meat into their pockets. Brynlee grabbed up a few fruits that looked good enough to eat that were sitting in a pile along with some packets of camping meals from the 21st century.

"Let's get out of here before he comes back," Carsen suggested.

"I don't know," Cameron said chewing on the side of his lip like his grandmother always did when she was thinking. "I think this guy can teach us a lot about how to survive."

"You're not suggesting we talk to him are you?" Brynlee raised an eyebrow.

"More like watching him from a distance," Cameron corrected her. "We need to stay close to him so he can show us what to do to get more food on our own."

"Yeah, and also when he talks to himself, he'll let us know what his next moves are," Carsen pointed out.

"And possibly what treasure he is after." Brynlee concluded.

Carefully, and as quietly as they could, the Biggs Bunch headed off down the same trail the pirate had taken, hopeful that they weren't making a big mistake.

CHAPTER 2
LIVING OFF THE LAND

For two days the Biggs children followed the pirate. Through his ramblings, they learned his name was Butch. Brynlee was insistent that it must be a nickname because no mother would name a cute little baby "Butch."

From watching the pirate, they learned where the water was. It was a quite a hike so it wasn't often they went for water. Instead, they used large leaves from the trees to catch the afternoon rain which seemed to be a constant companion for the island. Rain water, was barely enough to keep the children from getting too thirsty.

John Alexander Lott

On the first day after their arrival, Cameron and Carsen watched Butch as he reset one of his many traps made of wood and vines. The boys figured out that certain vines were stronger than others and could be used like rope. They began gathering those vines right after identifying them by watching Butch.

Brynlee discovered how to make even the weaker vines useful by weaving them together just like her hair braids. She sat back at their "camp" as the boys went out to watch Butch. They learned a lot from watching him. Once or twice they even swiped a bite or two of food from his stash.

The kids felt terrible about stealing the food. The hunger they felt during the first day without food was the worst thing they had ever felt before. After all, it was their second day without a meal.

For that reason, the boys watched the pirate very carefully as he set snares and traps. They did this for two reasons. First, they wanted to stop having to steal in order to eat. And second, they had heard about living off of the land in survival stories they'd read. Both boys were dying to learn how to do it for themselves.

On the second day, Carsen stayed back with Brynlee. Cameron went off to follow Butch alone. Carsen and Brynlee rigged up a shelter. They began by taking a long, straight stick about four or five inches thick, and tied one end of a vine to the stick about one foot from the center.

Next they threw the vine over a low branch of a tree about eight feet up off of the ground. Carsen wrapped the vine once around the stick before throwing the vine back the way it had come from around the tree, and up onto the overhead branch on the far side.

"The stick is on one side of the tree and the branch is on the other," Brynlee stated. "I don't get what you're trying to do."

Carsen explained. "I'm going to push you up onto that branch, and you are going to throw me the vine. I'll wrap it around the left side of the stick, and then throw it back to you. Then you pull it tight and throw the vine over the right side of the stick. I'll wrap it once and throw it back to you again. We repeat this pattern four or five times, as many times as the vine will allow. If we keep the vine tight, it should hold the stick right where we need it."

Brynlee was a little confused. "Are you planning to lean poles against the stick for us to sleep underneath? It would make more sense to just lean poles against the branch you want me to climb up."

"We're building a platform, Sis," Carsen explained patiently. "The roof will be made of those huge leaves. I want to sleep off of the ground, because we don't know if this island has snakes. I'm not willing to find out by having one decide to cuddle with me during the night."

Brynlee was the most helpful girl in the world after that. Cuddling with a snake didn't sound like a good idea to her either. She and Carsen had two poles lashed to trees and two more lashed to those poles in a rectangular pattern before Brynlee dared to question her brother again. It happened while she was down on the ground scrounging around for more wood.

"I thought we were going to lash more long poles together between these two trees," she called out to her brother who was tightening a knot on one of the poles.

"Nope," Carsen answered. "There are more of these shorter poles around than the longer ones, so the poles going between the trees will be our supports for the floor, and we'll lay the shorter poles crossways so they are parallel to the sticks we first tied to the trees."

Brynlee shrugged and trudged on through the undergrowth as she searched for more of the sticks and poles for construction.

By the time Cameron returned to their campsite, Brynlee was busily weaving a net of sorts out of the weaker vines. Carsen was rigging up the leaf roof over part of the new ten foot long platform. Cameron was very impressed with the work his brother and sister had put in .

"Wow, you guys didn't waste any time today did you?"

Carsen lowered the ladder he and Brynlee had made and Cameron climbed up to survey the finished product. He marveled at the sturdiness of the platform.

Carsen explained that the triangular shape at each end of the six foot wide platform was what made it stronger.

"I learned it watching that show where guys build those crazy simple machines to see if they can be used to do modern day jobs. What was the name of it again?"

"I don't remember," Cameron admitted. "But I know the one you're talking about."

"Right, well something about the triangle makes the whole structure stronger for some reason. I wasn't sure it was going to work, but check it out!"

Carsen jumped up and down two or three times to prove the strength of his knots. Again, Cameron was impressed.

"Nice job, little bro!"

"Thanks," Carsen shrugged.

"But why did you decide to build it so high off the ground?"

"Snakes," Brynlee answered quickly as she appeared at the top of the ladder.

Cameron, who didn't like snakes very much, shuddered as Brynlee began tying one end of her vines to a tree branch on one end of the platform.

"What if they can climb the trees?" Cameron asked, terrifying himself with the thought.

"Aaaand that's why I made this," Brynlee smiled as she began to tie off the opposite end of her creation to another branch from the same tree.

"Brynlee, aren't those the wimpy vines that don't hold any weight?" Carsen asked.

"Yep," Brynlee said with a grin.

"What did you make out of them?"

Brynlee finished tying her creation to the second branch and opened up her tangle of vines to reveal its purpose.

"You made a hammock?" both Biggs boys wrinkled their foreheads.

"I *wove* a hammock, yes," Brynlee replied beaming with pride.

Cameron and Carsen went on to explain that it was a cool idea, but she had chosen to use the wrong vines. During their lecture, they turned to speak to each other. As they turned back to their sister, they saw Brynlee calmly resting in the hammock, hands behind her head, a smug grin on her face as she waited for them to notice.

"What was that you said, boys? I couldn't hear you over the sound of my own awesomeness."

"It's gonna break," Cameron predicted.

"No it won't," Brynlee countered. "I braided three vines together to make them extra strong."

Carsen chimed in. "Alone each one is weak, but together the three are strong. Kind of like us, eh guys?"

Cameron smiled and nodded. He pulled out some fresh fruit he'd picked while watching Butch that day and filled in his siblings on what he'd learned from the ramblings of the pirate.

Butch was indeed his nickname, and he'd been given it during his time in the Marines. None of his outfit could pronounce his real name, first or last, so they called him Butch because, while not being the largest in the group, he was by far the strongest.

After leaving the Marines a decade ago, Butch got into a lot of trouble by gambling. It was the huge debt he owed to some very dangerous people that drove him to accept Vanessa's offer of mind-blowing wealth.

For three more days, the children spent most of their time improving their hut and listening to the old marine talk to himself. They learned Butch's target was a ship called the *Mary Dear* and that it was expected to arrive at any time.

Butch only had a rough estimate for when the ship could arrive, so he planned from the beginning to stay on the island for a long period of time, which was why he had brought so much with him from the 21st century.

One night, as the children lay in their hammocks, each made by Brynlee, they talked about a plan to get the locket and wand away from Butch.

"He never takes off the locket. Even when he goes for a swim in the pond by the spring," Cameron said.

"I've seen the wand tucked into his belt every time I've watched him," Carsen added.

"I feel bad that we're going to leave him here all alone on the island," Brynlee cut in. "It doesn't seem right."

"BJ, he is up to his eyeballs in debt back home, he has no family, and he actually enjoys the peace and quiet. He's said so many times over the past week."

"He's talking to himself in the middle of the jungle, Cam. It doesn't get much more sad and pathetic than that."

"I understand what you're saying, Sis," Carsen said sitting up in his hammock. "But the only other way to stop him is to convince him that his debts aren't a big deal and that he can give up on this whole idea of getting fabulously wealthy overnight. The odds of that happening aren't just not good, sis. They're impossible."

The three of them went into their own thoughts for the rest of the evening. Brynlee was the last to drift off to the sounds of the birds and insects of the jungle singing their sweet lullaby.

The next morning, the trio started off down the trail a little later than usual. Butch had arisen early in the morning as he always did. He packed his lunch and headed off to his perch in a tree at the southern edge of the island.

From there he sat and waited for the ship to arrive. He usually passed the time by dealing out several hands of cards to invisible players and played several hands of poker. He played the hand he dealt for each player and laughed hysterically at the same jokes he told to the imaginary players.

Cameron could just hear Butch's cackle as they were approaching the usual spot from which they watched him do his thing, when they all heard the laughter stop suddenly. The oldest Biggs held his hand up for the others to wait. Carsen and Brynlee fell instantly silent. Had they been seen? They didn't know.

Cameron crouched down and gestured for Carsen and Brynlee to do the same. Big brother turned to whisper something to the younger two when suddenly Butch came crashing through the ferns and vines in their direction.

Before Cameron could react, Butch tripped over the boy's body and fell face down in the dirt path right in between the younger Biggs' and their older brother.

The man leaped to his feet pulling out a gun and a knife. Carsen stepped in front of Brynlee to protect her. Cameron began to shout to get Butch's attention back on him, instead of his siblings.

The pirate's forehead wrinkled into a confused look as he whipped his head back and forth between Cameron and the other two.

"What are you kids doing here?" he shouted as he cocked his gun and aimed it between Cameron's eyes.

CHAPTER 3
AN ALLIANCE

"You look like something out of a western," Butch growled. "And the bump on my shin tells me I'm not imagining you. Explain yourselves!"

"We followed you here!" Cameron blurted out before anyone else could think of anything to say.

Carsen gave him a look behind Butch's back as if to ask *"Why in the world are you telling him that?"*

"We went into the cave when our little sister followed you guys, and we accidentally got sucked into that glowing orb."

Butch seemed to be working things out in his mind. He thought for a second and then asked a question.

"How long have you been on the island?"

"Only for a week or so," Cameron kept up with the honesty.

Butch grunted, "That explains where the jerky and other food went. I thought it was monkeys or something. I'm just glad it wasn't my mind slipping."

Cameron was hoping his honesty was buying them some time. He'd heard that a well-trained marine could tell when someone was lying to him. He wasn't sure if this was actually the case, but he figured it was better to be safe than sorry.

Carsen and Brynlee stood up slowly, wondering if they should be fleeing into the jungle. Carsen, who was just tall enough to see over the tall grass, noticed something white on the horizon.

It was a ship! That was why Butch had been running. The ship carrying the treasure he was after had finally arrived.

"I don't have time for this, kids. I'll make you a deal. I'm guessing you know why I'm here."

Cameron nodded.

"Well, I'll give you a share of the treasure to keep for yourselves if you promise to get it and get out of the tunnel before Vanessa returns from the place she went for treasure. I've done most of the work, so don't get any ideas about it being a huge amount of stuff. I can use the help, and I'm your only hope of getting back to our time."

Without another word, and without waiting for a reply, Butch got back to his feet and headed back toward his camp at a trot. The Biggs bunch followed at a slightly slower pace.

"I say we run for it," Carsen said when he was sure the pirate was out of earshot. "We could hide at the fort, or maybe . . ."

"He's former marine," Cameron reminded his brother. "I'm sure it wouldn't be too hard for him to track us down."

"Well I don't trust him," Brynlee said with a scowl.

"I don't trust him either, BJ," Cameron admitted. I just don't know what else we can do about it."

The children walked for a minute in silence each one trying to think of an idea to help with their current problem. They straddled a log in the trail, and reached out to each other to steady their balance as each one crossed it. As they neared the pirate's campsite, Cameron shared his idea with his siblings.

"Listen. Remember those cheesy kids adventure shows we used to watch all the time?"

Carsen and Brynlee nodded.

"Why were the kids always able to beat the adults?"

"Because it said so in the script?" Carsen said with a silly grin.

Cameron rolled his eyes and grinned at his brother's joke. "Yeah, but why?"

The other two shrugged.

"Because the adults thought the kids didn't really understand what was going on, and were too small and weak to be able to stop them. They overestimated them."

Carsen was trying to figure it out. "So you're saying we try to make ourselves look like easy targets?"

Cameron bobbed his head from side to side squinting as he thought of the right words.

"More like, a few innocent kids who aren't a threat to his plans because we don't know any better. Get the idea?" Cameron smiled slightly as his siblings faces began to show that they had caught on to what he was saying.

"Just some dumb kids?" Brynlee grinned, while tossing her blond curls to one side and then the other. "I think I can fake it for a day or two."

As the children arrived in Butch's camp, they found him scrambling to pack a few things into his cargo pants. A sharp knife was strapped to his leg just above his boot. Another was attached to his belt. Cameron wasn't the only one who noticed the gun tucked into the back of his pants. Carsen actually gulped his feelings out loud while Brynlee's eyes widened to show her thoughts.

"I figure they'll put down anchor in the bay just over the ridge. If we hurry we can get into position to watch things from a safe distance."

"How far away is a safe distance?" Cameron wondered.

"A couple hundred yards ought to be enough," Butch said tossing Cameron a pair of binoculars.

The children listened as Butch explained the basics of his plan, and the research he'd done in finding this island in the first place.

The Captain of the *Mary Dear*, a man named William Thompson, decided along with his crew, to turn pirate and steal a fabulous treasure they were supposed to be taking from Lima, Peru, to Mexico. Peru was having a revolution at the time. The Spanish decided to move the treasure so they didn't lose it to the Peruvians.

The treasure was collected by the Spanish over hundreds of years and included many things made of silver and gold, as well as jewels. The largest pieces were actually two solid gold statues of Mary holding a baby Jesus.

"They just trusted Thompson and his crew with all of that treasure?" Carsen asked.

Butch laughed a short, mean sounding laugh.

"Would you?" He continued without waiting for Carsen to reply. "There were guards posted and Catholic priests there to watch over the treasure too."

"And the priests and guards went along with the piracy?" Brynlee asked in amazement.

Butch glared at Brynlee as though she had three heads and slowly shook his head.

"Well then, what did they do . . . oh," the little girl gasped slightly as she realized the truth.

"Slitting throats and tossing a holy man overboard is easy for men like that to do," Butch grinned evilly. "What else would you expect from a pirate?"

Carsen swallowed hard again, reaching for his own throat.

"So what is your plan?" Cameron inquired.

"Well, the way I see it, we can watch the crew as they bury the treasure, wait for them to leave, and then dig it back up and bring it to the 21st century. Now that you're here, I'm willing to let you share in the spoils if you help me dig it up and promise not to let Vanessa know you were ever here."

Cameron wasn't buying it. "You're just one person, with only one shovel. How more much help could *we* be?"

Butch pulled back a tarp next to his cot and revealed three shovels.

"In my experience, you never go anywhere without a back-up or two of your most important tools."

"Still sounds too simple. What are you not telling us?"

"You ask a lot of questions, kid. Don't you know what curiosity does?"

Cameron gave a little half grin.

"Yeah, my grandpa uses that phrase."

Brynlee whispered her question to Carsen.

"What does it do?"

Carsen hadn't been following the conversation until Cameron's comment about the word 'curiosity.' He remembered his grandpa's phrase too.

"Curiosity kills cats. It's an old saying, I think."

Butch studied Cameron. "You're brave, kid. I'll give you that. And you're a smart one too. I do need you for something else. I want to hide part of the treasure in a different place, a place that Vanessa and the others don't know about. I got a sneaking suspicion that she's not going to be as generous as she let us believe she would be, and I want a back-up in case she double crosses me."

"No honor among thieves, eh," Cameron smirked.

"You had better hope there's not," Butch replied. "Vanessa told us to kill anyone who might discover our little secret. And when she says anyone," he leaned in closer and whispered as he continued, "she means it."

Cameron stopped smirking and fought the urge to run. Carsen went from gulping to whimpering, and Brynlee took over the gulping.

"You three aren't here on vacation, and you haven't responded to any of the secret signs of our group. I have been using them off and on for the past few minutes. So now I *know* you're not with the Time Pirates. I should kill you, and I could, but I won't if you'll agree to help me. That's the deal, take it or leave it."

CHAPTER 4
COMPANY!

Butch didn't wait for a reply from the shocked and frightened children. He just grabbed up his pack of supplies and a short handled shovel and headed off down the trail. Cameron turned to look at his siblings. They stared back, wide eyed and shrugged their answer to his unspoken question.

"So I guess we're Time Pirates now?" Carsen finally spoke.

Cameron shook his head, "Come on. We have to just go with it for now. He knows we're here and that we aren't with them officially."

The trio caught up with Butch as he was using binoculars to spot the ship on the horizon. He watched in silence as the boat drew nearer and nearer to the island. It was headed right for the small cove where the pirate had figured they would drop anchor.

As the small group watched and waited, Butch filled in some of the details about the history of the last days of the crew of the *Mary Dear*. After burying the treasure, they planned to split-up and meet again when the Spanish stopped looking for them. Unfortunately, they were caught anyway and all but the captain and his first mate were hanged.

"Captain Thompson made the authorities believe he would show them to the treasure in exchange for his life," Butch revealed.

"But they killed him anyway?" Cameron guessed.

Butch gave the boy an odd look.

"If he showed them the location of the treasure, then it wouldn't be lost anymore, would it? So why would I be here to steal it?"

"Oh!" Cameron nodded quickly trying to look like he didn't understand until it was spelled out for him. However, in a quick glance to his brother and sister he showed he was pretending with a wink and a grin. He was playing the part of an innocent and confused little boy perfectly.

Carsen couldn't help but wonder how long his brother had been able to hide such brilliantly disguised lying abilities. He wasn't sure whether he should be proud or worried. Brynlee was leaning toward proud.

Butch finally continued, "Thompson and the first mate led the Spanish back to the island, but disappeared into the jungle never to be seen or heard from again."

"So why didn't the Spanish look for the gold?" Carsen asked.

"They did," Butch explained. "But it was never found."

"Wait a minute," Brynlee said. "If they never found it, how do you even know the treasure is on this island?"

The comment drew stares from the other three. Cameron and Carsen gave her scolding looks as if to say, "Why are you trying to tick him off?"

Butch sent a snarl that basically said, "Are you trying to tick me off?"

"Maybe we should follow them to make sure they bury it here," Cameron said helpfully.

Butch grunted his agreement but added, "We need to stay out of sight and a fair distance away so they don't spot us."

All three kids agreed imagining the horrors that they might have to endure at the hands of evil pirates. Torture and death were not high on their list of thrill seeking activities.

The group of time pirates carefully made their way along game trails made by the smaller animals on the island as they followed the real pirates on their snakelike course through the jungle. Butch chose to stay on the higher ground in case they needed to run. He was very helpful to the children in avoiding the many snares and traps he had laid down to catch food.

The pirates hauled their sacks, crates, and barrels of treasure for a couple of miles into the jungle and then up the mountainside. They reached the base of a cliff partly hidden by a small waterfall.

Some of the crew started digging in the gravel while others began working together to move the larger rocks. A few were grumbling and complaining about the weight of the rocks.

Brynlee giggled at the funny swear words they were using.

"Be careful not to disturb much of the ground," commanded the man who was clearly in charge. "If anyone finds this place before we return, we don't want them having an easy time locating the treasure."

Cameron, who was looking over Butch's shoulder, suddenly stood up straight. He wore a look of confusion and his movement caught the Time Pirate's attention.

"What is it?" Butch whispered, although he doubted anyone could have heard him above the roar of the waterfall.

"Shouldn't the pirates be speaking Spanish?"

"Thompson is Scottish, and the crew are mostly British merchant sailors," Butch replied, still keeping his voice low. "I'm guessing a good number of them spoke Spanish, but they wouldn't have used it when they talked with each other."

The pirates were working hard and making quite a ruckus as they moved the giant rocks they would later use to cover up the treasure after it was buried. A few were gathering smaller stones to mix in with the dirt they were digging out of the hole.

One of the sailors brushed up against the canvas covering a large object that had been carried by no less than ten of the other sailors. The canvas fell away revealing a statue made of gold. It was a woman holding a baby.

"Is that Mary, holding baby Jesus?" Brynlee asked.

Butch could hardly contain his excitement.

"Yes," he breathed quickly as he spoke. "It was one of the objects that convinced me to go after this treasure in the first place. It's solid gold, and there are *two* of them. The other Time Pirates were very happy when I told them about it. It was those two statues that encouraged Vanessa to figure out ways to move larger objects than we could carry."

"Solid gold?" Carsen was amazed. "I'll bet that thing weighs a ton!"

"You're probably not far off," Butch agreed excitedly. "Boy wouldn't it be fun to see the looks on their faces when they come back and the treasure's not where they left it?"

Suddenly there was a thud. Butch collapsed to the ground, not moving. Cameron turned in time to see the butt of a gun racing toward his head. Carsen caught his big brother as he fell backward knocked-out cold. Brynlee screamed a piercing scream that let everyone within a mile know she was frightened. The larger Biggs was too heavy for the younger boy to hold for long, but Carsen let his brother down gently, and scowled up at the man responsible.

"What is it, then?" Thompson called out in his Scottish accent. "Find something did ye?"

"Aye, Captain," the sailor who had hit Butch and Cameron in the head called back. "A whole group of 'em."

The crew below began to bellow. Calls for execution rang out. Thompson quieted his men and demanded that the new prisoners to be brought down the hill to the edge of the pool below the waterfall. He ordered his men to keep digging. They complained that the island wasn't safe for the treasure anymore. He reminded them that they didn't have time to look for a better spot.

"A Spanish Man-of-war could find us any day, lads. Remember the guards, and the priests? The only hope for us is to not have the treasure with us if they find us."

Carsen stayed close to Brynlee as a small group of men surrounded them and picked up the two unconscious time travelers. Butch didn't stir, but Cameron came to as he was laid down before the captain. Carsen knelt next to his brother protectively and gave the men another angry scowl.

Brynlee joined in letting the men know exactly how she felt about them hurting Cameron. Her eyes narrowed to slits so close together that it was hard to see through them. She may have even stuck her tongue out.

William Thompson looked the three children up and down, noticing their clothes and their pale faces. Then he looked at Butch with his camouflage clothing and brown leathery skin. The captain was thinking long and hard before he spoke.

"This lot don't belong with him," he gestured to the unconscious man with a light tap with his own foot.

"Don't matter!" called out one of the pirates. "They've seen the treasure. I say we kill 'em and bury 'em along with it!"

"Aye" called another one. "Let their ghosts haunt any who come to look for it!"

The children shrank in fear as the pirates cackled with evil delight. Butch alone lay in peaceful slumber, and there was no one else within two hundred years and two thousand miles who could help them.

CHAPTER 5
SAVED BY THE BELL

"Would that include us when we return, then?' called a strong voice from behind the group. "Are we to be haunted by the ghosts of children over this bit of gold?"

The few pirates standing in the way parted and a tall man coolly stepped forward, a shovel still in his hand. His face was sweaty like everyone else, but his icy blue eyes were alive with a fire that made others take notice.

"Mr. Bell," Thompson began. "Something to say, have ye?"

"Aye, Captain."

"Well, let's have it. It has to be important, because in two years at sea with ye, I have yet to hear more than two words at a time come out of ye."

"I think it would be a mistake to kill them."

"And why is that, Mr. Bell?"

"Scavengers, sir, every island has them."

"Yes, I know that. What is it that you are getting at?"

"Well sir, if we bury the bodies here, scavengers will find them and dig them up. Now they don't have much use for treasure, but it would surely make the treasure easier to find for those who might come looking for it. And finding a body of any kind on a deserted island might cause the Spanish to look even harder, sir. We might not be able to come back for a while."

The captain was silent for a moment. It seemed he was wrestling in his mind with a difficult decision. All at once, his eyes brightened, as if he was getting a very good idea.

"We'll take them with us. There is plenty of time to deal with them later."

Guards were posted over Butch and the children while the crew continued digging into the heat of the day. Sometime after mid-day, the pirates moved the treasure into the hole they had created. They began the difficult task of reburying the loot and disguising the resting place so it looked like the surrounding area.

Carsen was skeptical that they could pull it off, but when they were finished putting the large rocks and the moss back, he had to admit, he would never have guessed there was anything buried there.

Cameron was moaning about his face. There was a large bruise covering much of the left side from his forehead to his jaw. Brynlee and Carsen did their best to comfort him. The blow delivered to Butch's head knocked him out cold.

The crew started marching back to the ships.

There was no one left on board. Captain Thompson didn't trust any of his crew enough to give them the chance to leave them on the island. Cameron, Carsen and Brynlee had to walk. Butch was carried in a litter with his hands and feet bound.

Once onboard the ship, the crew took very little time putting out to sea. Butch awoke during the row boat trip between the beach and the ship. A splash of cool ocean water had landed on his face. He sat up quickly and belted out a few curse words that caused Brynlee to giggle.

The kids and Butch were herded down into a metal cage in the lower levels of the ship. There were signs of water leaking into that level, and it made the kids nervous. Butch was left tied up because the sailors were so worried about getting as much space between them and the island as possible in case they were discovered by the Spanish.

When the guards were gone up to help the rest of the crew set sail, Cameron finally broke the silence.

"Well, at least we are still alive," the boy said hopefully.

"You're forgetting the history lesson I gave earlier."

"What history lesson?" Carsen asked.

"Didn't I tell you?" Butch growled. "The *Mary Dear* was captured by the Spanish a few days after burying the treasure."

Cameron felt a chill go down his spine. He didn't like where this history lesson was going.

"So now that we're aboard the ship, we are technically part of the crew, at least as far as the Spanish will be concerned."

"Why do I get the feeling that's not a good thing?" Carsen whimpered.

"Because piracy is a crime punishable by death," Butch paused to stress the last two words, "by hanging."

"Oh man!" Carsen whined. "I was almost liking this adventure before you said that."

"I'm leaving 1820 right now and going back to the cave to start over again. Now I know where the treasure is buried. I can use a different date and avoid the pirates altogether."

Butch reached inside his shirt to the locket, and pulled the wand out of one of his pockets in his cargo pants. He was leaving right then!

The Biggs bunch leaped for the man, still struggling against the ropes he was tied up in. Cameron grabbed the arm that was grasping the wand, while Brynlee and Carsen grasped for the locket's gold chain.

They struggled with Butch for a minute or two trying to convince him to stay. Brynlee was holding the locket with both hands and Cameron was using all of his body weight to keep Butch's other arm from connecting the wand and the locket. Carsen tried to reason with him.

"If you disappear, they might go back to the island and move the treasure to a different place. Maybe not even on that island anymore."

Butch stopped. "We've only got one night," he mumbled. "Vanessa said it couldn't wait for some reason."

Carsen knew he had chosen the right words, and wanted to really make his point.

"If they go back and move it, it's lost for good."

Butch needed no more convincing. Of course he knew what she would do. He told the kids that Vanessa was crazy enough and desperate enough to do almost anything to get her treasure. They realized they were going to have to figure out some other way to get home, *and* make sure that Butch didn't bring back anything to the 21st century.

CHAPTER 6
DINNER WITH THE CAPTAIN

The next night, Mr. Bell, the man who spoke up and saved their lives unlocked the door of the brig and told the children they had been invited to dine with Captain Thompson.

"Great!" Butch exclaimed. "I'm starved!"

"Not you, sir," Mr. Bell stated firmly. "Just the children."

Butch grumbled angrily under his breath as Cameron, Carsen, and Brynlee stepped out to freedom. He continued to complain until they were out of earshot.

"I don't think he's very happy with us right now," Carsen mumbled to Cameron.

"I just hope he doesn't do anything foolish like use the wand to go back to the mine shaft," Cameron whispered back.

The children were led to the back of the ship, or the stern as Mr. Bell called it. The door on the main deck was opened from the inside. They were led into a dark, candle-lit room. There was a table and four chairs set up with a platter of dried meat, another of questionable fruits, and a third full of rolls.

"Welcome, my young friends," the captain said smoothly. "Please, sit down."

"Thank you, Captain," Cameron said as he and his siblings took seats around the circular table.

"I'll admit, that I have had reservations about bringing ye on board, but I am a curious man."

"Well, you know what curiosity does," Cameron replied, trying to be funny.

"Curiosity drives a man to discover new worlds, and to seek for that which is of value to him," responded the captain, a little confused by Cameron's comment.

Cameron quickly realized that the phrase "curiosity killed the cat," probably came about after 1820, the time they were currently in.

"Of *real* value, or what he *thinks* is of value," Cameron said, repeating something he'd heard in a movie. He wasn't sure what it meant, but it sounded good and the wise old man from the movie sounded good saying it.

Captain Thompson nodded his head in agreement.

"You are wise beyond your years, young mister . . ."

"Biggs," Cameron replied. "Cameron Biggs. This is my brother, Carsen, and my sister, Brynlee."

"The pleasure is mine."

"May I ask a question, Captain?"

"You may, indeed, Mr. Biggs," the captain smiled as he picked up a few pieces of meat and a couple of rolls from the platters. "But please take some food for yourselves. You must be hungry."

Carsen and Brynlee reached for the food while Cameron continued talking.

"A day ago you were ready to kill us and bury us on that island. Why are you so nice now?"

"A captain must maintain the trust and respect of his crew," Thompson said as he took a huge bite from a piece of meat.

"I'll admit though, the thought crossed my mind that I should do precisely as the crew implored."

Brynlee was having a hard time hiding her disgust at the food flying out of the captain's mouth as he spoke. She turned to look away as she bit into a roll. It was hard and tasteless, but she decided it was food, and kept quiet about it.

"So why didn't you just do it?" Cameron asked, remembering what Butch had told them about what the pirates had done to the men who had been guarding the treasure.

Carsen wanted very badly to elbow his brother in the ribs, but he was too far away. It sounded to him, like Cameron was egging the captain on, just daring him to complete the evil deed!

"I told ye, lad. I'm a curious man. It appears to me as though ye have no real connection to that man with which we found ye."

Cameron nodded. "That's right, we barely know him. We just met on the island."

"And for what purpose were you on the island, then?"

Cameron chewed his lip again. Honesty had been his approach with Butch, but he was having a harder time telling the truth this time around.

"We weren't supposed to be there," Carsen chimed in, his face stuffed with dried meat.

"When we left home, we didn't know that was where we'd end up," Cameron told the captain.

"Stowaways, are ye now?"

"Something like that," Cameron grinned.

The meal went on for a minute or two and the conversation stopped for a moment. Then Cameron picked up a roll, tore it in half, and slipped a piece of meat in between the two halves. Thompson grinned as he commented on the 'sandwich' saying that he'd only seen people eat like that once or twice before.

"Magellan!" Thompson called. From the dark shadows came a dog wagging his tail and panting.

A piece of meat was thrown in the dog's direction. Magellan caught it in mid-air and happily scarfed it down.

"Why did you name him gelatin?"

Cameron laughed. "It's Magellan, sis. He was an explorer. Members of his crew were among the first to sail around the world, even though he died in the Philippines during the voyage."

The captain was impressed at Cameron's knowledge. He gave him a nod of approval as he chowed down on another roll.

Brynlee got down off the chair and sat on the floor next to the dog. She played with it for a while as the captain explained his plan to avoid being captured by the Spanish. Cameron, remembering a book he once read, suggested that a disguise for the ship might help them sneak around unnoticed. Thompson liked the idea and called for Mr. Bell to begin right away on a disguise for the ship.

At the end of the meal, the kids got up from the table, and were about to leave when they were called back.

"Why is it, my young friends, that you have chosen to take my hospitality as an opportunity to steal from my table?"

"What?" Cameron and Carsen gasped.

"I don't miss much, lass."

"Brynlee!" Cameron scolded.

"It's for Butch," Brynlee defended. "I know we can't trust him, but he's probably hungry too."

Carsen, pulled out another roll and a piece of meat as well. He admitted that he had the same idea.

The captain laughed. "Ye three are truly not like any other stowaways I've ever met. Off with ye now and feed the poor beggar." He laughed once more as the children left the room.

For the next couple of days, the crew was busy disguising the ship with paint and tar and whatever else they could think of. They hoped to make it not look like the *Mary Dear* who stole the great treasure of Lima. The Biggs children were given free run of the ship, but Butch remained confined to the brig because the captain didn't trust him.

Cameron couldn't figure out why Captain Thompson trusted the kids more than Butch. He puzzled on that every day. There had to be more going on than the captain was telling them.

Brynlee went everywhere with Magellan. Or maybe it was the dog that never left Brynlee. It was fast becoming an unbreakable friendship. They ate together and slept together. Brynlee called him Mage for short, and she wouldn't listen to anyone who told her Mage sounded more like a female name.

Once they saw a ship on the horizon. It was identified as a Spanish warship called a Man-of-War. The crew was very nervous for the few hours that they were being followed by the warship. All breathed a huge sigh of relief when it finally disappeared over the horizon again.

On the night before they were planning to arrive at a small trading port in Costa Rica, the Biggs bunch visited Butch in the brig, bringing him his dinner. He wasn't in a good mood.

"I offered to make you partners and give you wealth you'd never dream of, and you pay me back with betrayal."

"I hear you've been spitting and cursing at the guards who bring you food and water," Cameron replied.

Butch shrugged, "So what?"

"So, I bet you'd have an easier time gaining their trust if you were nice."

"It won't matter much anyway. I'll be hanging with the rest of the crew in a few days."

"You don't belong here in the 1800s. You have my word, Butch. I will not let you hang," Cameron vowed.

Early the next morning, the cry of land was raised by the look out. Brynlee was the first to the railing to look toward the rising sun hoping to catch a glimpse of land. She hadn't been doing very well with sea life and was excited about being back on land again.

After a few minutes of watching as the little port grew ever larger on the horizon, she noticed a few members of the crew were standing nearby with their hands on their knives. She thought it was strange, but was distracted by the sights of the other ships in the harbor. Among them was a large Spanish Man-of-War like they had seen earlier.

Cameron and Carsen came to the deck and were only a few steps behind their sister, when suddenly they were grabbed from behind and thrown hard to the wooden deck. Their hands were being tied behind their backs. Brynlee whirled around in time to see Carsen's chin bleeding from a cut that appeared when he hit the hard wood.

"Get the girl too!" Brynlee heard someone shout.

Brynlee took one look out to the approaching harbor, and judged it to be a couple hundred feet away. A hand grabbed at her arm. Mage snapped his jaws at the hand, and the sailor changed his mind. Brynlee only had a second to make a decision.

"Run BJ!" Cameron shouted.

Brynlee tried to flee but found herself cornered, so instead, she climbed through the railing and jumped overboard. The splash of cool water would have been refreshing if she hadn't been so terrified. Her pioneer style dress, now soaked with water began to weigh her down. She undid the buttons at the back of her neck, and slipped down and out of the dress. Her pajamas were more form fitting, and while heavier, did not slow down her swimming strokes.

She heard a splash behind her and turned, horrified that someone was coming after her. There was Mage, happily dog paddling in her direction. Brynlee called to the dog and kept swimming for shore. She turned once more and noticed that Cameron and Carsen were being hauled below decks. She could only guess that they were being thrown back into the brig for some reason.

The frightened little girl bravely made her way to shore. She climbed out of the water scurrying into the town by the early morning light in her dripping wet pajamas. She was alone, but she was free. Now she had to figure out how to survive on her own.

CHAPTER 7
NARROW ESCAPES

"This is what you get for double crossing me," Butch sneered.

"They think *I* double crossed *them*!" Cameron said rubbing the goose egg the guards had given him.

"I'm pretty sure they overheard us talking last night and misunderstood," Carsen said still holding a piece of his shirt against the cut on his chin.

Butch was about to reply again, when they heard a terrible shriek above deck. The sounds of men scrambling and shouting were everywhere. Gun shots were heard. It took several minutes for the noise to subside. At about that time, armed men entered the area of the ship where the captives were being held. They took one look at the three time travelers and called for their commander.

A stuffy looking man in a sharp uniform descended the ladder and approached the brig. After a minute or two of silence, he ordered the prisoners to be held with the rest of the crew.

Cameron and Carsen were too frightened to realize that the captain had been speaking English. Butch noticed but kept quiet until later when they were paraded through the streets of the small town toward a stone building. It looked like an old fortress and there were cannons on the roof.

"Am I the only one who noticed the Spanish guards were speaking English?" Butch whispered to Cameron, as they walked with their hands on their heads.

"So what?" Cameron whispered.

"They didn't even have an accent."

Cameron nodded thoughtfully.

"Maybe they're just good at English," the boy suggested.

"The captain, maybe," Butch replied. "But the regular soldiers too? I don't think so."

"Am I the only one who wouldn't care if they were speaking Chinese?" Carsen whispered impatiently. "We are being marched to our death and you two are arguing about their language!"

"Keep quiet English dogs!" One of the nearest guards barked.

"Sorry," Carsen whimpered.

"Look here!" laughed the guard. "One of the pups speaks Spanish!"

Cameron raised an eyebrow. "He does?"

The guard stopped short and stared at the boys for a minute. "Lock them up for now, but go get the general. These children might be stowaways from Lima."

While her brothers were busy trying to figure out why the guards thought they were speaking Spanish, when it sounded like the guards themselves were actually speaking English, Brynlee was changing into her nice warm new clothes. A white pullover and a colorful skirt were just the thing to keep her disguised. She also wore a kind of wig she had made out of the hair from a doll to hide her blond hair.

Mage had been wearing a silver dog collar which Brynlee used to trade for the clothes and a few other odds and ends. She took her precious cargo along as she introduced herself to the parents of the new friend she had made that day in the market. They seemed as though they weren't even paying attention. It was probably just as well. She had very little time. She was hoping and praying for a miracle, but was still working to complete her plan as though everything counted on her.

Cameron and Carsen were spared from the questioning because it was still assumed that they could be Peruvian, or even from one of the wealthy Spanish families living in Lima at the time of the revolution. They sat in silence as the crew grumbled and argued or sat with dazed looks thinking about their upcoming trial. It wasn't likely that they would see too many more sunrises, and each man knew it.

For two days the crew was imprisoned within the damp stone walls of the fortress's dungeon. The keys to the prison doors were kept by the guards who came and went with the prisoners for interrogation. The lone guard in the dungeon was only there for extra crowd control when the cell doors were opened.

The pirates were only taken out for a few minutes at a time as the Spanish were trying to force them to tell where they had buried the treasure. Each time the door to the prison was opened, everyone cowered in fear of being next. It seemed that they were going to be able to stay alive only if they could keep from giving away the treasure's location.

Then, late in the evening on the second day, the door opened again. The guard took his eyes off of the grumbling pirates and turned to face the end of a wooden pipe. A spray of liquid came bursting out the end and into his eyes. The poor man shrieked in pain, and dropped his weapon. He staggered backward right into the bars of the prison. His cries had alerted the pirates who turned to see Brynlee snatching the powder horn hanging from the guard's belt. They grabbed at the guard from behind and pulled hard. His head hit the bars and he was out cold on the floor.

"Get back!" Brynlee yelled as she crammed the powder horn into the tiny space between the iron bars and the stone wall at one end of the prison cell.

Knowing the power of black powder, the sailors and time travelers all scrambled for the far end of the cell. Brynlee pulled a fuse out from her little pouch and lit one end with a couple of strikes from a piece of metal and a rock.

"Where did she come from and how the heck did she know how to do any of that?" Carsen shouted with his hands clasped over his ears expecting the explosion of the powder horn.

Cameron didn't have time to reply. The walls of the small prison shook with the force of the explosion. Dust and smoke filled the air and men began coughing. Everyone's ears were ringing from the blast. Brynlee ran over to the blast site only to find that the explosion had only dislodged a single stone. By pushing it back into the cell, a narrow opening was revealed.

Brynlee was visibly disappointed in the effect her 'bomb' had on the stone walls.

Cameron looked at the pitiful results of the explosion. "Well that was anti-climactic."

"Anti what, now?"

"Not as impressive as I thought it would be," Cameron clarified.

Carsen was already wiggling through the narrow opening. Cameron, a little larger than his brother, was having trouble squeezing through the space. With Brynlee and Carsen tugging on one end, Cameron finally fit through the hole and breathed sigh of relief.

The trio turned to look at the doomed men behind them. There was nothing more they could do. They didn't have any more black powder, and the hole in the wall wasn't large enough for a man to fit through.

"Just go, you fools!" Butch shouted. "You still have a chance to get home!"

The guard on the floor stirred. He groaned and shouted a cursing.

The children called out their wishes of good luck to the crew as they scurried down the stone hallway into another part of the fortress. The guards, who entered, began laughing as they saw the prisoners' glum faces staring at the pitifully tiny hole left by the explosion.

A searching party was sent out to discover any threat, as the stunned guard was replaced by two others. They couldn't help but keep chuckling at the plight of the doomed pirates and the failed jailbreak. They seemed to totally forget about the children.

When things quieted back down, Butch's shoulders slumped. He was trapped. The Spanish had confiscated his locket and wand. He was as far from home as he'd ever been in his entire life. Yet his mind never stopped working on the situation. He was constantly going through details trying to figure out how get free and save his own life. His combat and survival training had prepared him for this very moment. Of that, he was sure.

All at once an idea came to him. It sat there a moment rolling around in his mind before he spoke aloud. It was crazy, but that was why the old marine loved it so much.

"Captain Thompson," he called over to the sad looking man. "I wonder if I might have a word with you."

Butch laid it all out for the captain in low tones off to one side of the group. He didn't reveal who he was, only that he had an idea about how to escape. He ought to have had one. He had read everything there was to know about the treasure during his research.

His goal was no longer to steal the treasure for himself. He wanted to become part of the legend. In fact, he was convinced that it was the only way he was going to survive.

"Make me your first mate, Captain. We tell them that together we'll lead them to the treasure, but take them to a different island."

"Won't work," Thompson said immediately. "A few of the crew have already told them which island we buried it on."

Butch chewed on that for a minute.

"I know that island pretty well, Captain," he bragged. There are plenty of places to hide. I will help you if you cut me in on the treasure."

It was Thompson's turn to chew on the new information. The idea of, not only surviving the day, but also of possibly still having a chance to keep the treasure was tempting.

Butch added one more thought to sway the captain in his favor.

"We can die here like dogs, or we can roll the dice and possibly live like kings for the rest of our lives. Things can still work out in our favor, Captain. The choice is yours."

CHAPTER 8
A DECISION TO MAKE

The Biggs bunch ran from the fortress avoiding any and all official looking people. It was still too early to get dark which meant it wouldn't be very easy to hide. They scurried through the streets of town and toward the harbor. The boys were following Brynlee because she seemed to know where she was going.

As they ran, she filled them in on what she'd been doing for the last few days. She described grinding hot pepper seeds to dust and mixing them with a light cooking oil to make the 'pepper spray' she had used on the guard.

The boiling hot oil along with the pepper powder worked perfectly. She had used a single wooden tube from a broken pan pipe to hold the homemade pepper spray, and to blow it into the eyes of the guard.

Cameron and Carsen gaped at their little sister and then at each other as they ran out onto the docks.

"Sounds like they're searching for us," Carsen stated, tilting his head off to one side.

"We can hide under the docks," Cameron guessed. "But we gotta hurry. It sounds like they're getting closer.

Shouts and the sounds of footsteps were indeed getting nearer to the children. Together they climbed down beneath the wooden planks forming the top of the docks. They were careful not to fall into the water.

Only once in the next hour did soldiers even come out onto the dock, and that was only for a minute because it was easy to see that no one was about.

The dock Brynlee had chosen didn't have any ships moored at it. They were either out in the harbor, or tied up at the other dock.

Cameron and Carsen complimented their sister on her quick thinking. She suggested that they get new clothes. Carsen thought they ought to use Brynlee's locket and wand to go back to the mine shaft. Brynlee disagreed.

"What if someone accidentally figures out what to do with the locket and wand?"

"The odds of that happening are not great, BJ."

"But can we really take that chance?" she countered. "I say we go back and get the other lockets and wands so we leave no doubt about the treasure being safe from the Time Pirates."

"When did you start making so much sense?" Cameron teased.

"I've always made sense," Brynlee sassed. "You boys just never paid attention before now."

Brynlee climbed out first, since she was the least likely to be recognized by searching eyes. When the coast was clear, she beckoned to her brothers.

"Hurry, I think we need to get you two a disguise, and the market is about to close."

"How do you know that?"

"Duh," she responded with a shake of her head. "The sun's going down soon!"

Brynlee led the way through the quiet, dusty streets to the shop owner who sold her the clothes she was wearing.

"Ah, my little golden haired friend," said the man with a pleasant smile. "What can I get for you today?"

"My brothers need a change of clothes."

"Well, I think I still owe you for the silver from the other day. Come on back and let's have a look at my fine merchandise."

The boys kept their pants and shoes, but donned new pullovers like ponchos. They also bought hats to cover their light colored hair. The kindly old man prepared a stash of food with tortillas and some papaya, bananas, and other odds and ends to eat.

"For the dog," the shop owner said with a smile as he packed away a large piece of dried meat and a bone.

With their disguises complete, and some food for their bellies, the children made their way back toward the town square. They overheard some guards talking about the prisoners, and listened carefully.

"Sounds like the captain and first mate are selling out the rest of the crew."

"What do you mean?" Brynlee asks.

"They just said that the whole crew will be hung tomorrow, but that the captain and first mate are going to lead them to the treasure."

"What do you want to bet, Butch is now the first mate?" Carsen challenged.

"Seems like something he would do," Cameron agreed.

"So do we go back now or stay to make sure Butch doesn't get away with the treasure?"

"Good question, Carsen. I think we have to stay."

"If we do that, then we have one more stop to make before boarding the ship," Brynlee stated.

"What ship?" Cameron wonders.

"The Man-of-War that they just mentioned. It's out in the harbor. I saw it earlier today. They just said it was the ship that would lead the recovery efforts for the treasure."

"I must have missed it," Cameron said as his sister walked off down a different street. "Where are you going?"

"You'll see!" Brynlee called back without turning.

Time Pirates

CHAPTER 9
A LOCKET FOR EVERYONE

Brynlee led the way turning around corners all of a sudden as though she was trying to remember where to go. The boys followed in silence, but noticed the sun dropping nearer to the horizon. They hoped their sister knew what she was doing.

"Where are we going again?" Cameron asked.

"Back to the fortress," said Brynlee casually.

"What?" Carsen shrieked before quieting himself. "We just escaped two hours ago, and you want to go back?"

Brynlee didn't answer; she just darted out behind a loaded cart being pulled by a donkey. She kept walking alongside the cart as it made its way down the street. Cameron and Carsen couldn't understand what she was doing until they saw the soldiers forming ranks around two men exiting the prison in chains. It was clear even from a hundred yards away that the two men were Thompson and Butch.

Cameron and Carsen dove for the back side of the next passing cart. They followed their sister's lead as they kept the cart between themselves and the soldiers. They especially didn't want Butch or Thompson to notice them.

"Just so you know," said a voice nearby with a thick Spanish accent. "All of your guards speak English so there won't be any miscommunication, you British dogs."

"I've learned my lesson, lad. The Spanish are too clever for my liking. I won't let myself be outwitted by them again. We'll keep our end of the bargain so long as your men keep theirs," Thompson spoke in a voice filled with defeat.

"Thompson's a good actor," Cameron whispered.

"Yeah, I bet he's never been defeated in his life," Carsen said.

At the corner of the street, the boys joined their sister in laying flat against the wall.

"Took you guys long enough," Brynlee said impatiently.

"We stopped to see the sights, okay? It's our first time in Costa Rica," Cameron retorted.

"Where is Costa Rica anyway?" Brynlee asked with a quizzical look.

"I'll show you on a map when we get home, now let's get what we're here for and get the heck out of here!" Carsen pled.

Brynlee led the boys up a stone staircase at the side of the fortress. She explained that this was the commander's home. She opened up a heavy wooden door at the top of the stairs and invited the boys in.

From there they went across the room to another doorway leading into a narrow corridor. Down the hall, there was a medium sized door with new brass hinges and paint on it. Brynlee opened that door. As it fell open, the trio could see light from the small window shining on the prize of all prizes.

"The lockets!" Cameron exclaimed rushing forward.

"And the wands too!" Carsen said joining his brother at the table in the center of the room

"How in the world did you know they were here?" Cameron demanded with a surprised half grin on his face.

"Girls have secrets," Brynlee replied with a toss of her hair. "And mine include a friend I made while I was hiding in town. The commander's daughter is about my age. She helped me heat the oil and crush the seeds from the peppers that I used to blind the guard."

"When did you become so 'cloak and dagger,' sis?" Carsen spoke with awe and wonder to his little sister. "I'm impressed, really."

Brynlee blushed at the compliment, but added. "I stayed with Rita for two days, not on the streets. I had a lot of help from her and the servants."

Just then a young girl entered cautiously. She smiled when she saw Brynlee.

"Hello again my friend," she said as she embraced Brynlee.

The girls ended the hug quickly as the girl began talking. The members of the crew of the *Mary Dear* were to be executed at dawn, but the captain and first mate made a deal to lead the

Commander and his men to the treasure in exchange for their lives.

Brynlee confirmed the identity of the ship they would be taking and promised that they would do everything in their power to stop the pirates from getting away with the treasure.

"Be careful, and have fun hunting down the rest of those Time Pirates!" Rita exclaimed.

The boys' eyebrows shot up as they followed their sister out the door and back to the street.

"You told her about us?" Cameron complained.

"Well how else was I going to get the daughter of an officer in the Spanish navy to trust me? I told her about our quest to stop the Time Pirates so she could see we're the good guys. I needed help, and with you two behind bars things weren't looking very peachy. Besides, who was going to look after Mage while I was rescuing you two?"

Magellan sauntered in and covered Brynlee's face in dog kisses.

"I'm just impressed you got her to believe that story," Carsen grinned as he patted the dog on the head.

"Well, I left out just enough details to make it a little more believable. She loves the idea of magic though, so that helped," Brynlee winked.

As it turned out, there were three ships going on the journey back to the island. Thompson was loaded onto the first and largest, and Butch was loaded onto one of the two smaller ships. The children watched the soldiers and sailors loading the ships as the sun set.

"I say we get on that third ship," Cameron explained. "I don't want to risk bumping into Butch *or* Thompson during the trip."

"Good idea," Carsen agreed. "Security is probably going to be more relaxed on that third ship too."

"This is going to be so exciting!" Brynlee squealed. "I've never been a stowaway before!"

Being a stowaway wasn't nearly as exciting as Brynlee thought it would be. For three days they basically slept and hid under canvases covering boxes of food. Carsen and Magellan hid between barrels of water. Their slender builds allowed them to slip quietly between and behind the back three barrels in the cargo hold. The men were only drinking from the front barrels so they never had to move.

Brynlee and Cameron on the other hand, had to constantly find new places to hide every few hours as the next meal was prepared. It seemed like they always chose to hide behind the wrong stack of food. After two days Brynlee was convinced they were going to starve.

"We polished off the last of the food from the market yesterday, and there is nothing but flour, dried peppers, and water in this part of the hold!"

"Quiet down, BJ," Cameron scolded gently. "We have to be getting close to the island. We'll raid Butch's stash of jerky, trail mix, and instant oatmeal before we leave for the mine shaft."

"We'd better get there quick," Carsen grumbled sticking his head out from behind the barrels. "You two are starting to look like drumsticks."

Cameron snorted out a quiet laugh. "Yeah, I'll bet I could use this flour and water to make a paste to roll you in. Then I'd cover you with some crushed peppers and make some hot wings!"

The children all began to laugh a silent, shaky laugh.

"Land ho!" called a man above deck.

"We're there," Cameron breathed a sigh of relief. "Let's get planning."

"What kind of plan?"

"We need to stop Butch from bringing anything back, but also protect the treasure from the Spanish so history doesn't change. Otherwise Butch will have researched an entirely different treasure, and everything we've done was for nothing. We would still need to go stop him."

"Like playing video games with someone who keeps restarting if things don't go their way," Carsen groaned.

"Exactly, so let's do it right."

Time Pirates

CHAPTER 10
BACK TO THE ISLAND

The landing party from each ship planned to leave before dawn. The Biggs' plan was to leave before then to make sure they got to a good hiding place before the Spanish could see them. They left early in the morning for shore while the stars were still lighting up the night sky.

"If anything goes wrong, use the locket to go back to the mine shaft," Cameron commanded as he checked both of his siblings for their lockets.

Carsen wore Tiny's locket. Brynlee wore the original one which Carsen had found back in the mine, and Cameron now wore Butch's.

Borrowing a small dingy attached to the stern of the ship, they rowed as fast as they could for shore. Cameron and Carsen had never felt so grateful for a crazy scout leader who demanded that all cub scouts learn to row a boat and paddle a canoe.

By some miracle, the kids made it to shore and were able to hide the boat in the thick greenery near the beach. They used branches to brush away their footprints in the sand as they backed into the shadows of the trees. Brynlee turned on the flashlight from Cameron's phone to light their way.

"Where did you get that?" her brother asked in surprise. "I thought I'd lost it when we were following the pirates to the burial spot."

"I swiped it from your pocket the night before when I climbed down from the treehouse to go to the bathroom."

"For the first time in my life, I am going to thank you for stealing my phone," Cameron said with a grin. Then the grin turned into a scowl. "But don't ever do that again."

Without knowing where Butch and Thompson were going to lead the Spanish on their wild goose chase, the children positioned themselves near the beach where they could just barely see the boats as they came in, They were far enough away to be able to scramble for safety over a ridge if they needed to.

"Do we have time to go for food?" Carsen wondered.

"Probably not," Cameron admitted. "They'll want to get an early start so they don't have to keep track of all of the loot at night."

"Here they come!" Brynlee shouted.

"Brynlee, I hope this is the last time I ever have to tell you to keep quiet when we are in danger," Cameron's voice was oozing with stress and tension.

Brynlee realized her mistake and covered her mouth with both hands.

"Sorry," she meekly said.

The children watched through the trees as the boats made their way to the beach. They could just overhear Thompson and Butch explaining the distance they would need to travel to get to the treasure's resting place. They described in detail the narrow trails and trees they would need to climb over to get there.

"You can leave our shackles on if you like," Butch was saying. "But the hike is fairly strenuous, and a man cannot make it where we are going while restrained."

"Personally, I'd prefer it if you carried us the whole way," Thompson added with a snicker in his voice.

Their shackles were removed, but awful threats were made that would later give nightmares to the children. The trek made slow progress at first. Thompson claimed it was hard to find the same trail, but the general direction they were traveling was correct.

The children followed carefully along a trail on higher ground. The thick vegetation was high enough the Mage was hidden completely from view, and only Cameron had to duck much to stay hidden. As the men in the narrowing canyon below began to climb upwards toward the children, they backed off even more choosing to stay just under the ridge.

"We could set off some of Butch's traps to help them," Brynlee suggested.

"I don't think he has any set in this area, and even if he does, we can't find them in time to set them off. Butch will have to lead them into the traps by himself," Cameron whispered back.

"How will we know when it's safe to go home?" Carsen asked.

"I think we owe it to Butch to give him the chance to come with us," Cameron said.

"Why?" Carsen whisper screamed.

"I am beginning to think that Vanessa just chose troubled people to be Time Pirates because she knew she could control them. Maybe not all of them, but I think Butch deserves the chance to change."

"I think you're crazy," Carsen stated.

"Watch your step," Butch called out as he held back a springy branch hanging over the trail.

Cameron was confused as he watched the men snake their way along the trail about fifty feet below them.

"He's helping them," he whispered to his brother and sister.

Butch pointed out a few large rocks in the trail hidden in the undergrowth. "There's more where these came from. If you tripped, it could be a nasty fall down a steep slope like that." He gestured down into the narrowing ravine.

"I don't understand why he's helping them," Brynlee whispered.

"Maybe he's trying to get on their good side," Carsen suggested. "If that many angry men had guns pointed at me, I'd be looking for any way I could think of to get them to like me."

"I think we need to watch from a little bit farther away," Cameron said quietly, still confused about Butch's actions.

The Biggs bunch moved higher up the mountainside toward the saddle that they knew led to the other side of the island. The tree house and Butch's campground were located there. The Spanish commander was starting to question the route they were taking when Butch held back another branch and pointed at the ground around the man's feet.

As soon as the commander looked down for the rocks, Butch let the branch spring back into place which knocked the Spaniard backwards and sideways a little. The force of the branch hitting him wasn't hard enough to hurt much, but it was more than enough to cause him to stumble off of the trail. He screamed in panic as he began tumbling down the steep mountainside hitting rocks, vines, and tree roots as he rolled.

Butch and Thompson were twenty yards away before any of the soldiers realized that the swinging branch hadn't been a mistake, and that their prisoners were trying to escape. Shots rang out echoing off of the narrow canyon walls, but none of them hit the fleeing pirates.

"Don't kill them, just wound. We still need them to lead us to the treasure!" shouted the second in command who took over for his boss even before the commander stopped screaming. The poor man was still falling down the mountainside, but no one was coming to his rescue.

Carsen led the way as the Biggs clan tore through the vines and ferns. Brynlee was close on his heels and Cameron was bringing up the rear keeping one eye on the trail behind them looking for either Spaniards or Butch and Thompson. Carsen soon spotted the trail leading from Butch's camp to his look out spot on the mountain. He altered the direction of their flight, but the blinding speed of their kicking legs did not change.

By the time Cameron arrived at Butch's camp, Carsen had already taken Butch's spare gun from its hiding place, unloaded it, and was just placing it back. Brynlee was picking up the bullets and putting them in her pocket. Cameron grabbed up Butch's last bag of twenty-first century trail mix, and kept on going right on through the camp.

"Butch and Thompson won't be far behind us. I think we should hide."

"Now you want to hide?" Carsen sighed.

"Yeah, I forgot he still had a gun here on the island. If he is still mad at us, I'd like to have the edge of him not knowing we are even here."

The children hid in the same large patch of ferns that they fell into when they first came to the island almost a week and a half earlier. Not three minutes later, Butch entered the clearing followed by Thompson. Both men were panting and sweating.

Butch knelt down and picked up two bottles of water. He threw one to Thompson and reached back down to his pack. As the captain figured out the screw-on lid of the plastic bottle, Butch picked up his gun and aimed it at him.

Thompson didn't notice until he had nearly drained the entire water bottle. When he saw the object in Butch's hand he was confused. He had never seen a gun from the twenty-first century, but he knew what Butch was doing.

"You dog!"

"Ouch, that really hurts," Butch said sarcastically.

The time pirate went on for a minute or two about his plans for the treasure. He had no intention of returning to his time anymore. It would be so much easier to live like a king here in the 1800s.

"You swine!" Thompson snapped. "If I didn't want to leave any of the treasure with the Spanish, what makes you think I'd want to share any of it with you?"

"What you thought doesn't matter, because I have this," Butch sneered as he pulled the trigger.

Nothing happened.

Butch pulled the trigger again, but still nothing. He began to inspect the gun when Thompson picked up a large stick from the wood pile and hefted it. He noticed the look in the captain's eyes and threw the worthless gun at him, as he dove for another branch.

The children watched with surprise as the two men fought each other with the sticks. Each made a few hits on the other's body, but at times missed horribly until all at once, they both connected with each other's heads and knocked each other out cold.

Cameron's head poked up farther out of the large fern in which the Biggs were hiding. He watched the two unconscious men for a few seconds before stepping out into the clearing. Carsen followed.

"Well, that ended quickly," Carsen remarked.

"Boys are so dumb sometimes," Brynlee said shaking her head.

"Eh, sometimes," Cameron agreed. "I kind of think money does that to a lot of grown-ups."

"Well, you heard Butch," Carsen said. "He doesn't want to come home with us."

Magellan walked over to the captain and licked his face. The man began stirring. Butch was waking up as well.

"What do we do now?" Carsen whispered.

"I think we need to leave him here like we left Tiny. He can survive, and without a locket and wand, he's no longer a threat to us."

"I guess that means we each get to keep a locket for now," Brynlee smiled.

"How the devil did you get back on this island?" Butch screeched as he sat up, rubbing his bruised head.

"Does it matter?" Thompson hissed. "Listen, you can hear them searching for us!"

The captain sprang for the jungle crashing through the undergrowth.

"Let's go!" Carsen said grabbing his wand and locket.

Cameron paused. "Butch, I gave you my word."

Butch nodded. "I know you did, kid. And you're the only person I've ever known to keep it. But I can't go back. With no treasure, there's *nothing* for me there."

Cameron nodded back. "I don't feel good about leaving you behind."

"Don't worry about it. If Thompson and I can give these Spaniards the slip,

we just might make it out of here. Even
if he gets himself caught, I have a few
hideouts where I could lay low until they
give up looking."

Butch thought for a moment before
adding. "Vanessa is a really bad egg.
You have to stop her."

"We could use some help with that,"
Cameron admitted.

Voices calling out orders, and other
replying that a trail had been found,
floated in the jungle. Butch and
Cameron were both wondering the
same thing.

Why were the Spaniards calling to
each other in English with no accent?
Butch turned to look at Cameron and
the others one last time.

"You go, but if you really need help,
you know where to find me," he said
with a determined look on his face. "I
gotta make sure Thompson doesn't get
away with the treasure either."

With that, the time pirate was gone.
As Cameron approached his siblings,

Carsen looped his locket around all three of their heads, and touched it with the wand.

Magellan came bursting out of the ferns, tail wagging and tongue flapping. As the children disappeared, the dog leaped into the void along with them.

CHAPTER 11
A NEW FRIEND

The tunnel of swirling lights held four individuals this time. Brynlee squealed with delight as she saw Magellan. Carsen reached out and grabbed the dog around the middle. Cameron, who still wasn't too fond of the feeling of falling, tensed up all of his muscles as they traveled back to the mine shaft.

The four of them burst onto the hard rocky floor of the mine laughing and wrestling with Magellan who wasn't sure what was going on. Cameron was the first to rise to his feet. Carsen then stood next to his brother. The glowing blue orb was still lighting up the rocky walls of the room, giving them an eerie look.

"We could still go get help," Carsen offered as he noticed his brother staring at the orb with a worried look on his face.

"We still don't have enough proof to get anyone to even follow us into the shaft in the first place," Cameron reminded him.

"And even if we did, the returns for each of the pirates are set five minutes apart," Brynlee sighed. "There are a bunch of them who could get back and get away before we found help."

"So it's on to the next?" Cameron asked looking at his brother and sister. "There's more danger ahead."

"Bring it on!" Carsen said sticking out his skinny chest.

"Mage and I are ready," Brynlee stated, her fists placed firmly on her hips.

As if in agreement, Magellan barked happily.

Cameron looked down at the tablet controlling the power of the orb.

Next Destination? It read.

Cameron bent over and selected the next destination by pushing 'OK.' Then he used his own wand to open up the next portal. The energy surge was intense.

The boy's arms were shaking from the strain of lifting the wand. It was like the pull of the invisible stretching rubber bands had doubled in strength. He was grunting and lifting with all of his might when Brynlee and Carsen ran forward and jumped into the crack in the fabric of time.

Magellan was less enthusiastic about another trip through the portal, but with a little coaxing from Cameron, took the plunge. Cameron gave one last heave upward to make sure he had enough room to duck through the opening, and fell sideways into the portal.

Cameron watched as he fell behind his siblings. Magellan looked terrified with his tail sticking straight out. The dog howled long and mournfully. It was almost as if he was able to sense the dangerous adventure that lay ahead.

The sound caused Cameron to consider that the obstacles and pirates they had faced so far were nothing like what lay ahead.

ABOUT THE AUTHOR

John Alexander Lott grew up playing in the orchard behind his house in Orem, Utah. As a child he spent hours dreaming up adventures for himself and the other neighborhood children. His favorite subject in school was history. He loved learning about different times and dreamed of visiting them to see what life was like there. He could often be found reading about the new and exciting things he had heard about at school.

John began writing stories as a way of living out his daydreams. He encourages his readers to have a dream, write it down, make it happen, and then find another dream to work on.

Check out John's other books, on his blog at quickstepuniverse.blogspot.com, and don't forget to "like" the Quickstep Universe, the page for all of his stories, on Facebook.